Treasure Hunt

Look out for more
mermaid adventures:
Pirate Trouble
Whale Rescue
Spooky Shipwreck

Mermaid Rock

Treasure Hunt

Kelly McKain
illustrated by Cecilia Johansson

■SCHOLASTIC

Scholastic Children's Books,
Euston House, 24 Eversholt Street
London NW1 1DB, UK
a division of Scholastic Ltd
London ~ New York ~ Toronto ~ Sydney ~ Auckland
Mexico City ~ New Delhi ~ Hong Kong

First published by Scholastic Ltd, 2004
This edition published by Scholastic Ltd, 2006

10 digit ISBN 0 439 95112 7
13 digit ISBN 978 0439 95112 8

Printed and bound by Tien Wah Press Pte. Ltd, Singapore

10 9 8 7 6 5 4 3 2 1

☆ Chapter One ☆

It was an ordinary day on Mermaid Rock.
Coralie and Shelle were singing and
combing their hair.

"Come on, Spirulina, join in!" they cried.

"But it's boring," grumbled Spirulina.

"I wish I could have an adventure instead."

WHOOSH!

Suddenly a chariot pulled by two giant sea horses came thundering towards them.

"It's Father!" Spirulina cried.

Neptune's chariot skidded to a halt, splashing his three daughters from top to tail.

Spirulina giggled – she loved sea spray. But she soon stopped laughing when she saw the sad look on Neptune's face.

"Oh, my darlings, I bring terrible news," he boomed. "I lost a bet with Ariel and now I must give him all my treasure."

The three sisters gasped with horror.

"No treasure?" cried Coralie.

Neptune hung his proud head. "It's even worse than that. My treasure's been stolen! Now Ariel says that I must find it by sunset or he'll take the Floating Palace instead."

"No palace?" shouted Shelle.
Spirulina's sisters began to scream and sob.

"What terrible news, Father!" said
Spirulina. "But don't
worry. I'll find the
treasure before sunset.
You won't have to
give the Floating
Palace to Ariel."
Neptune hugged
Spirulina tenderly.

"My brave little one," he said, "you mean well, but what can you do? You are only a fragile mermaid. I shall go and prepare to leave my beloved palace."

With that, he leaped aboard his chariot and swept off over the sea.

"He's right," wept Shelle. "There's nothing you can do."

"We'll see about that," grumbled Spirulina, who did not like being called little or fragile. "The treasure must be hidden somewhere."

She stood up on her tail and looked around, but all she could see from Mermaid Rock was a broken fishing rod on the beach.

Just then, she glanced up and spotted Ariel's Sky Castle, floating high above on its cloud.

"I bet I could see for miles from one of those turrets," Spirulina cried. "I'd be sure to spot the stolen treasure then."

"But how will you get up there?"
asked Coralie. "Mermaids
can't fly!"

"Wait and see," said
Spirulina, winking.

She swam over to the shore and collected
the broken fishing rod. Then she fetched
her tool belt and set
to work. Soon it
was as good
as new.

Spirulina swam back to Mermaid Rock
and showed the rod to her sisters: "I'll hook
the Sky Castle with this
rod," she explained.
"Then I'll reel
myself up."

"Don't be stupid,
Spirulina!" sniggered Shelle.
"You'll never manage that!" cried Coralie.

☆ Chapter Two ☆

Spirulina stood on the very tip of Mermaid Rock and cast up at the Sky Castle. But no matter how hard she tried, the fishing line wouldn't go high enough. Even worse, the Sky Castle had nearly floated out of reach.

"It won't work!"
shouted Shelle.

"Give up now!"
called Coralie.

But Spirulina kept
on trying until…

"Yes!" She was suddenly pulled into the
sky! She looked up and gasped in surprise…

…she hadn't hooked the Sky Castle at all! Instead, she'd hooked an albatross!

"Please could you take me to the Sky Castle," she called.

"I'm not taking you anywhere," said the albatross crossly. "In fact, I'm going to shake you off in a minute. I'm not a taxi service, you know."

Spirulina gulped as she swung around on
the fishing line. It was a very long way
down. She felt ever so frightened.

"Oh, please help me," she cried. "I'm on an important mission. You see, someone has stolen my father's treasure. I must find it before sunset!"

"My, that really is important," said the albatross. "Okay, climb aboard and I'll take you to the Sky Castle. You can call me Albi."

"I'm Spirulina," panted Spirulina, scrambling on to Albi's back. She hooked the fishing line on to her tool belt.

A few moments later they reached the Sky Castle. "Hold on tight," called Albi. "It might be a bumpy landing!"

With a crash and a bang, Spirulina and Albi touched down on top of one of the turrets.

Ariel, who had been busy inside the castle, heard all the noise and flew out to see what was happening.

"What are you two doing up here?" he demanded.

"We're looking for the stolen treasure," Spirulina explained. "You don't mind, do you?"

Ariel laughed. "Mind? Of course not! Good luck to you!" And with that, he flew back inside.

Spirulina and Albi grinned at each other, and started the search for the stolen treasure.

☆ Chapter Three ☆

Spirulina and Albi hurried from tower to tower, looking in every direction. They peered far out to sea and all along the coast, but there was no sign of the stolen treasure.

"Oh, dear!" said Spirulina. "I really thought we would see it from up here."

"Don't worry," said Albi. "Let's fly around and take a closer look."

Albi's idea made Spirulina feel much more cheerful.

They swooped down off the turret...

...and checked the upturned fishing boats and the lighthouse, but there was no stolen treasure.

They searched all day,
peering deep inside
craggedy caves...

...and digging up sandy beaches in case
the stolen treasure had been buried.

But there was no sign of it anywhere.

Just as the sun was beginning to set, Spirulina and Albi landed on top of the Sky Castle once again. They took one last sweeping look, but there was still no sign of the stolen treasure. They were both exhausted, filthy and utterly miserable.

Just then, Ariel flew up to them.

"Have you found the treasure yet?"
he asked.

"No,"
Albi admitted.

"Oh, what a
shame!" said Ariel.

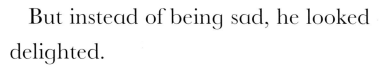

But instead of being sad, he looked
delighted.

"I shall have to take the Floating
Palace instead."

"Please, Ariel, don't take my father's home," begged Spirulina, starting to cry.

But Ariel just laughed.

"A bet is a bet. Now, do excuse me. It's only a few minutes till sunset. I have to get to Mermaid Rock to claim my new palace."

"What a wicked sprite!" squawked Albi, when Ariel had flown away. "But it looks like the palace will be his after all. We've searched everywhere! We'll have to give up."

"Don't say that!" said Spirulina, drying her eyes. "We must keep looking."

As the sun sank lower it shone straight on to the Sky Castle.

Suddenly Spirulina spotted something glinting in the tiny, barred window opposite.

"Look over there!" she gasped. "I think I can see something."

Albi peered at the window. "It's probably nothing," he squawked sadly, "but climb aboard, and we'll take a closer look."

Hardly daring to hope, Spirulina and Albi swooped across to the window, landed on the wide ledge and peered inside.

☆ Chapter Four ☆

"Father's treasure!" cried Spirulina.

"Shh!" hissed Albi.

There was a mean-looking guard sitting right next to the pile of jewels. Spirulina and Albi bobbed down just as the guard turned round.

"Ariel stole the treasure himself!" whispered Spirulina crossly. "What a sneak!"

"But why would he do that?" whispered Albi. "He's won it anyway."

Spirulina thought hard. "Yes, but this way he gets the Floating Palace too! Then he'll rule the sky *and* the sea. He'll banish Father for ever. Oh, Albi, we have to stop him!"

"You're right!" squawked Albi. "We must rescue the treasure – and fast! The sun has almost set! But we can't get in through these bars."

Albi looked defeated, but Spirulina grinned. "*We* can't. But this can," she said, unclipping the fishing rod from her tool belt.

"Good idea!" squawked Albi. "We can fish for it! But how can we get rid of that guard?"

"Leave it to me," said Spirulina. "For once, my boring old mermaid skills will come in useful."

Spirulina leaned close to the window and began to sing softly.

Go to sleep, go to sleep, go to sleep, great big guardie. You are snoring, you are snoring, to this boring mermaid song.

Spirulina sang the song over and over. Soon the guard fell into a deep slumber.

"Wow, how did you do that?" asked Albi.

"Mermaid lullabies send humans to sleep," Spirulina explained. "Okay, time to go fishing."

She cast the line through the window, snagged a pearl necklace and reeled it in.

CLINK!

The necklace hit the iron bars. Spirulina froze, afraid that the guard would wake up. But he just snorted and went back to his dreams.

Piece by piece, Spirulina pulled the treasure out of the window and piled it on to Albi's back.

"The ... sun ... has ... almost ... set ..." panted Albi, struggling to balance under the weight of the treasure. "H ... h ... hurry!"

"Just one more thing," said Spirulina, casting off into the gloomy room.

Spirulina heaved at the line. "This
diamond tiara is ever so heavy," she panted.
"That's … no … diamond … tiara …"
gasped Albi.

Quick as a flash,
Spirulina grabbed the tiara, stuck her
tongue out at the
guard and
leaped on
to Albi's
back.
"Let's go!"
she cried.

As the guard raced towards them, Albi launched off the windowsill and flapped his wings as hard as he could. But instead of zooming away, they just hung in the air. The treasure was far too heavy.

"Ahhhhh!" they screamed, spiralling downwards.

☆ Chapter Five ☆

While Spirulina was busy rescuing the treasure, Ariel had arrived on Mermaid Rock, to claim his winnings.

"Spirulina hasn't found the stolen treasure," he told Neptune, "even though I was kind enough to let her look from the Sky Castle. So you must give me the Floating Palace instead."

Neptune's shoulders drooped as he pulled a chain from his thick belt. The chain held the keys to the Floating Palace. Coralie wept and Shelle wailed as the sun vanished from the sky.

But just as Neptune was about to hand over the keys ... it began raining treasure!

"Hooray! The treasure is found!" cried Coralie as diamond tiaras, pearl necklaces and sapphire rings fell around them.

"Father, the palace is saved!" squealed
Shelle.

But Neptune was staring up at the sky
in horror. "My little one!"
he croaked.

Spirulina and Albi were falling fast, heading straight for a crash landing on Mermaid Rock.

Albi flapped hard, but they kept falling.

"I'm going to dive into the sea," cried Spirulina, "then you'll be able to fly out of harm's way!"

"No!" squawked Albi. "It's too dangerous!"

"Don't worry, I'll be fine," said Spirulina, although she felt really frightened.

She crossed her
fingers for
luck and then
leaped off
Albi's back.
SPLASH!

Spirulina bobbed to the surface just as Albi landed safely nearby.

Neptune beamed with relief. Coralie and
Shelle clapped their hands
in delight.

"Oh, my daughter, thank goodness you're safe!" bellowed Neptune. He bent down towards the water and lifted Spirulina up in his strong arms.

"And you found the treasure!" cried Coralie. "Just in time!"

"It was Albi too," said Spirulina.

"Well done, both of you," boomed Neptune. "But who stole it?"

"He did!" cried Spirulina, pointing at Ariel. "It was a trick to get the Floating Palace!"

"WHAT?" roared Neptune.

Ariel backed away from the furious sea king. "I m-m-must be going now," he stammered, and flew off.

"I'll deal with him later," Neptune promised. "Tonight there will be a party in honour of Spirulina and her new friend, Albi!"

Coralie and Shelle cheered and hurried off to tell all the creatures of the sea.

The party was held at the Floating Palace. There was music and dancing, fireworks and a huge cake.

Neptune raised a goblet of fruit punch. "A toast!" he bellowed, "to Albi and my brave daughter, Spirulina!"

"To Albi and Spirulina!" everyone cried.

Albi squawked with happiness, but Spirulina just smiled and sipped her punch, wondering what exciting adventures tomorrow would bring.